This book belongs to

____

Published by Advance Publishers

Written by Ronald Kidd
Illustrated by Adam Devaney and Diana Wakeman
Produced by Bumpy Slide Books

ISBN: 1-57973-000-0

10 9 8 7 6 5 4 3 2

THE PERFECT PARTY

Mrs. Potts had a bad case of the winter doldrums. The birds had all flown south. The ground was covered with a thick blanket of snow. And a cold, lonely wind whipped through the trees.

Her friends were in the doldrums, too. Chip was tired of being cooped up. Belle had read so many books to the Beast that her throat was sore. Cogsworth was barely ticking, and Lumiere's flame had lost its flicker.

There was only one thing to do. It was the same thing Mrs. Potts always did when she wanted to cheer people up. She decided to throw a party.

She promised herself that this wouldn't be just any party. It would be the most wonderful party ever given, the crowning achievement of her career.

Mrs. Potts gathered all her friends together to tell them the news. They were as excited as she was — in fact, all of them wanted to help.

"You're welcome to lend a hand," she told them. "There's certainly enough for all of you to do."

Mrs. Potts was busy cooking when the first helper arrived. It was Cogsworth. He surveyed the kitchen and declared, "See here, this place is completely disorganized! How do you expect to get anything done?"

Mrs. Potts stammered, "Well, I . . ."

"Never mind," said Cogsworth. "I can see

you'll need my help if you are to get this party off the ground."

He bustled about the room, moving things from place to place. "Pans in the cupboard? Nonsense! Anyone knows that pans go in the pantry. And just look at this food — it's not in alphabetical order!"

Finally Mrs. Potts could stand it no longer. "Thank you for helping, Cogsworth," she said firmly, "but I think I've got *everything* under control now."

She showed him to the door, then rearranged the kitchen the way it had been. Then she sighed. She was already *exhausted*, and her work had barely begun!

A few minutes later, Lumiere stopped by the banquet hall. He said, “Excuse me, Madame, but if I may say so, you look a bit tense.”

When Mrs. Potts explained, he said, “What you need, Madame, is a few moments’ rest.”

He poured a cup of hot tea to calm her nerves. Then he drew the curtain, shutting out the harsh daylight and replacing it with the soothing yellow glow of his candles. "You know," Lumiere murmured, "a lady as beautiful as yourself should never frown. It puts a chill in the air."

He poured a cup of tea for himself, and soon they were talking and laughing together. But as he leaned toward Mrs. Potts, one of his flames touched a stack of napkins, setting it on fire. Lumiere was having such a good time that he didn't even notice. "Ah, my dear Mrs. Potts," he said, "now the chill is gone. In fact, I'm beginning to feel quite warm!"

In the hallway, Belle was playing with Chip and Footstool when she smelled something burning. Then she saw the smoke coming from the banquet hall!

"Fire!" she cried, and went running inside.

Belle pulled the tablecloth, napkins and all, onto the floor. Then she tried to stamp out the flames. "Chip! Quick! Get some water!" she cried.

Chip hopped to the kitchen and returned with the water. But instead of throwing it on the fire, he missed and it ended up on Belle instead.

Meanwhile, Footstool raced in circles around them, barking wildly. Lumiere decided it might be a good time to leave. He slipped out the door.

After she put out the fire, Belle checked to make sure Mrs. Potts was all right. "Is there anything else I can do?" Belle asked.

"Yes, dear," replied a miserable Mrs. Potts, looking at the charred curtain. "Would you please bring in some wood for the stove?"

Belle put on her coat and made trip after trip to the woodpile, with Chip and Footstool following close behind. When she finished, there was a neat stack of wood next to the stove — and three sets of muddy footprints across the floor of the kitchen.

"My beautiful floor!" cried Mrs. Potts.

Belle said, "Here, let me — "

"Never mind," interrupted Mrs. Potts. "I'll take care of it, dear. But would you please take those two off to play somewhere else?"

The Beast arrived as Belle and her small friends were leaving. "Do you need some help?" he asked Mrs. Potts.

"Well," she said, "I suppose you could clean the floor."

He got down on his hands and knees and began to scrub without complaint. Amazingly, he finished the job without anything going wrong!

Mrs. Potts was so pleased that she asked for the Beast's help with the flowers. They went to the greenhouse and picked flowers of every color. Then the Beast put them into an array of beautiful glass vases and carried them back to the banquet hall.

The Beast walked carefully, trying not to spill the water on the newly washed floor. But before he could reach the table, Chip and Footstool came dashing in, playing a spirited game of tag.

"Watch out!" cried the Beast. But the two were already dashing around his legs, making him lose his balance.

"Look out!" cried the Beast as vases flew in all directions.

"Let me help you clean this up," the Beast said to Mrs. Potts.

"No! That's all right!" she exclaimed. "Please, no more help!" With that, she shooed him out of the room and slammed the doors.

The doors stayed closed all day. Late in the afternoon, Belle and the rest of the group gathered outside.

"I can't see anything!" said Belle. "But Mrs. Potts must still be planning on giving the party. Listen to all that clattering and clinking!"

At precisely six o'clock that evening, the doors swung open, and Mrs. Potts stepped out. She looked exhausted.

"Good heavens," said Cogsworth, "are you all right?"

"I'm fine!" she replied, sounding a little cranky. No one knew what to say. It was so unlike Mrs. Potts not to be cheerful. "And now, if you please, come inside. The perfect party is about to begin!"

The banquet hall had never looked more magnificent. On the table, china gleamed, silverware shone, and crystal glittered in the soft candlelight.

Cogsworth turned to the others and whispered, "No mistakes! Understand? Let's do our part to make this the perfect party."

And that's just what they did. They minded their manners. They sipped their drinks politely. They were careful not to spill or drop or smudge.

They always said please and thank you. In fact, that's about all they said, because they were trying so hard to be perfect.

Of course, there were a couple of close calls, such as when Lumiere almost dripped hot wax on the tablecloth, and the time the Beast lost hold of his fork and it went flying into the air.

Luckily, he caught it before it did any damage. All in all, though, everything went beautifully during the soup, the salad, and the main course.

When it was time for dessert, Mrs. Potts and Belle went into the kitchen. A few moments later they returned with the most exquisite cake anyone had ever seen. “I hope you enjoy this,” said Mrs. Potts. “I worked on it all afternoon.”

Everyone gathered around to admire the cake.
"Oh, boy!" Chip exclaimed. "Chocolate!"
"Never have I seen a finer cake," announced Cogsworth.

"Bravo, Madame," said Lumiere. "This is truly a masterpiece!"

Exactly what happened next will be debated for years to come. Some say Belle simply stumbled. Others claim she slipped on the newly waxed floor. No matter what caused it, Belle tripped, and the cake sailed off her tray.

As they all watched in horror, the top of the magnificent dessert made a great arc — and came to rest on Cogsworth.

The others gasped. They all turned to gaze at Mrs. Potts, sure that she would burst into tears. Belle felt awful. "I'm sorry I ruined your perfect party," she said to Mrs. Potts.

Then Mrs. Potts did something surprising! She started to laugh!

"Perfect?" she said. "This is the dreariest party I've ever been to, and it's all my fault. Enjoying the unexpected — that's what makes life fun. Why, if you ask me, a flying cake was just what this party needed!"

Everyone laughed and talked as Mrs. Potts and Belle cleaned Cogsworth off and served what was left of the cake. When they had eaten enough, the friends pushed back the table and began to dance.

As Mrs. Potts spun around the floor with Lumiere, she finally began to relax and enjoy herself for the first time that evening.

It may not have been the perfect party she had been hoping for — but it certainly was a lot more fun!

Everyone makes
His share of mistakes,
From spelling words wrong
To lopsided cakes.
Some make a few,
Some make lots and lots,
Some hate when they happen —
Just like Mrs. Potts.
But if everything always
Turned out perfectly,
How dull and boring
Each new day would be.